OVER THE MOON

BY RACHEL VAIL

ILLUSTRATED BY SCOTT NASH

ORCHARD BOOKS
NEW YORK

For D.J., Fathomer – R.V.

To Gibby with Love – S.N.

Hi Diddle Diddle,

The cat and the fiddle,

The cow jumped over the moon.

Hi Diddle Diddle,

The cat and the fiddle,

The cow jumped over the moon.

Hi Diddle Diddle,

The cat and the fiddle,

The cow jumped over the moon.

Hi Diddle Diddle,

The cat and the fiddle...

*H*i Diddle Diddle,

The cat and the FIDDLE,

The cow jumped over the moon.

I did it! I did it! Wa-hooo! I jumped OVER the MOON! HI! OVER! Hi? Hey, where's that Diddle Diddle guy?

Library of Congress Cataloging-in-Publication Data.   Vail, Rachel. Over the moon / by Rachel Vail ; illustrated by Scott Nash.
p.   cm. Summary: Hiram Diddle Diddle and a violin-playing cat encourage a cow to keep jumping until she makes it OVER the moon. ISBN 0-531-30068-4.—ISBN 0-531-33068-0 (lib. bdg.) [1. Cows—Fiction. 2. Cats—Fiction. 3. Characters in literature—Fiction.] I. Nash, Scott, date, ill. II. Title. PZ7.V19160v 1998 [E]—dc21 97-21964 10 9 8 7 6 5 4 3 2 1